Complete your Fireman Sam DVD Collection!

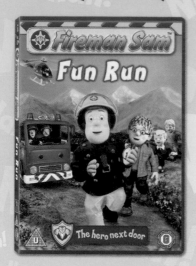

Coming soon!

The Big Freeze

is available to own from winter 2006

For more information please visit www.firemansam.co.uk

This Fireman Sam Annual belongs to

....

Annual 2007

Contents

Stories adapted from original scripts by Nigel Crowle, Marie Davis, Stan Hey, Holly Lyons, Robin Lyons, Andrew Offiler and Annie Smyth

EGMONT
We bring stories to life
First published in Great Britain 2006 by Egmont UK Limited
239 Kensington High Street, London W8 6SA

ISBN 978 1 4052 2609 7
ISBN 1 4052 2609 9
10 9 8 7 6 5 4 3 2 1

HiT ENTERTAINMENT S4C RHYNGWLADOL INTERNATIONAL

Meet Fireman Sam and his friends

Pontypandy is a friendly place where everyone knows everyone else. You might think that nothing much happens there – but you'd be wrong. There are all kinds of emergencies and rescues for the Pontypandy Fire Service to deal with!

Fireman Sam is the fireman who drives Jupiter, the fire engine. He's brave and always stays calm, even in a crisis. He's a real hero!

Sam likes inventing things in his shed and his house is full of his inventions. One of them gets him washed, dressed and ready for work in seven seconds flat!

Sam's a very good friend and neighbour and is always on hand to help.

He's a brilliant uncle to the twins, Sarah and James.

"Leave it to me, I'll see what I can do!"

Station Officer Steele is in charge of the Fire Station. He likes everything to be just right and always does things by the rule book. He's very proud of his firefighters and knows they're a great team.

"ACTION STATIONS!"

Penny Morris drives Venus, the Pontypandy rescue tender. She's also a mechanic and just loves to keep fit. Penny's idea of a great day is a long hike in the hills to do some rock-climbing and abseiling with her friend, Tom Thomas.

"You can do it! Go, girl, go!"

Elvis Cridlington is the Fire Station cook who overcooks everything – even salads! Elvis likes to look really cool and he loves listening to loud rock and roll music!

"Rock and roll!"

"Sam's forgotten more about rescuing people than I'll ever know."

Tom Thomas is in charge of the Mountain Rescue Station on Pontypandy Mountain. He's the pilot of the bright orange rescue helicopter, and drives the rescue jeep.

Mike Flood is the Pontypandy odd-job man. He can fix and mend just about anything. Mike loves helping people and he's a volunteer with the Mountain Rescue Service. He plays steel drums and has made his own kit from old boilers!

"And now for my drum solo!"

Helen Flood is married to Mike. She's the nurse who looks after everyone in Pontypandy. She's always out and about in her little white car. Nurse Flood helps Sam and Tom in emergency rescues.

"I LOVE reggae music!"

Dilys Price runs the only grocery shop in Pontypandy, so she knows everyone in the village. She always has time for a cup of tea and a chat, especially if it's with Trevor. She just loves her son, Norman.

"Who's Mummy's little darling?"

Trevor Evans drives the Pontypandy bus. He takes the children to and from school, runs the bus service to Newtown, and makes deliveries all over the village. He loves to stop for a chat with the ladies!

"I'll just have a nice cup of tea."

Bella Lasagne owns the café that is the main meeting place in Pontypandy. Everyone goes there for a coffee or a pizza – and a chat. Bella has a big voice, and a big heart. Her café is a little bit of sunny Italy in Pontypandy.

"Mamma mia! It's-a disaster!"

Meet Sam's young friends

Sarah is Sam's niece. She's very sensible and well-behaved and she always looks neat and tidy. The mums in the village wish their children were just like her!

"Be careful, James!"

James is Sarah's twin brother. He loves trying out new things and is always ready for fun and adventures. James is always asking questions and he can be a bit stubborn sometimes.

"Cool, let's do it!"

Norman Price is Dilys's son. He lives with his mum in a flat over the grocery shop. Everyone calls him 'Naughty' Norman because he's always playing tricks and pranks – and just being naughty!

"Norman's the name, being naughty's the game!"

Mandy Flood is Mike and Helen's daughter. She loves having adventures and sometimes gets her best friend Norman into trouble, even though she doesn't mean to. Her mum says she's a bit of a tomboy.

"I'm an act-now-think-later girl!"

... and the Pontypandy pets!

"Meow!" "Woof!" "Baa!"

Rosa is Bella's cat. She likes climbing trees and jumping into wells and holes. She's always getting into scrapes and has to be rescued by Sam.

Dusty is a stray dog. He doesn't belong to anyone, so he visits every house in the village looking for what he likes best in all the world – food.

Woolly is Norman's lamb. They've been friends since they both got stuck on a mountain ledge and had to be rescued by Sam and the team.

Nee Nah! Nee Nah!

Jupiter the fire engine isn't the only thing in Pontypandy that makes a lot of noise. So do the animals!
Can you point to Dusty, Woolly and Rosa and make the noises they make?

Baa! Woof! Meow!

Bug-eyed boy from Venus

One dark night, Fireman Sam was showing Sarah, James and Norman how to use his telescope.

"Point it over there," said Sam. "To the planet Venus ..."

"Venus!" said Norman. "Bug-eyed monsters live there!"

Just then, a bright light lit up the sky. "It's a shooting star," said Sam.

"No! That was an alien spaceship," said Norman. "From Venus!"

Next day, when James, Sarah and Norman were on their way to school Norman spotted a crop circle. "Look, it's where the aliens landed!" he told them.

"There's no such thing as aliens," said Trevor Evans, the bus driver.

"We'll see about that," whispered Norman.

After school, Norman went to Bella's café. He covered his face in green mushy peas and put on a silver foil cape and helmet.

"Arrrrrrr!" wailed Norman in his best alien voice.

"Arrrrrrr!"

14

News of the "alien" soon spread. When Trevor saw it heading for Pontypandy Mountain he told James and Sarah.

"Come on!" said James. "We'll catch him!"

Norman was running along when he slipped off the path into a muddy bog. He tried to get out, but he sank deeper and deeper into the black mud.

"HELP!" he cried, as Trevor and the twins arrived.

"HELP!"

"I'm stuck!" cried Norman. "Get me out of here!"

Back at the shop, Dilys was so worried about Norman that she rang 999. "My Norman's been taken by aliens!" she reported.

Sam got the message, pressed the alarm and the bell started ringing. "Aliens?" he said. "Likely story! But we'd better send out a search party."

Jupiter and the Fire Station crew were soon out on the road and at the Mountain Rescue Station Tom Thomas lifted off in the helicopter.

ACTION STATIONS!

Trevor knew how dangerous the bog was. He lay flat and told Sarah and James to hold on to his legs as he stretched out his hand to Norman.

"Hurry up, Mr Evans," said Norman. "My pants are filling up with mud!"
"It's no good, I'm sinking!" said Trevor. "Pull me back! We need help!"
As he spoke, the helicopter's blades whirred above them and a searchlight swept the sky.
"Over here!" cried Trevor.
Minutes later, Tom winched Sam up into the air then lowered him down over the bog. Norman was very pleased to see him!

Sam put a harness under Norman's arms. "I've got him!" he shouted to Tom. "Take it away!"

The helicopter rose up into the dark sky, with Sam and Norman in tow.

"**SQUELCH!**" went Norman as he was pulled free from the mud.

Dilys and Bella were waiting in the park when they saw the helicopter's lights.

"It's the spaceship that took my Norman!" said Dilys.

Seconds later a strange shape appeared in the darkness.

"It's-a hideous!" said Bella. "It's-a terrifying! It's-a ..."

"**NORMAN!**" said Dilys as he and Sam stepped out of the shadows.

"Yes, one green alien, safe and sound!" said Sam.

"My little precious!" said Dilys, giving Norman a big kiss.

"Oh, Mam!" said Norman. "Yuk!"

There's only one Fireman Sam ...

Or is there? These pictures of The Hero Next Door look the same, but if you look very carefully you'll see that only ONE of them is the real Fireman Sam. Can you find him?

1

2

3

4

5

Sarah took these photographs of Sam, Elvis and Penny with her new camera.
Can you find two photos that are exactly the same?

21

Smile, please!

Sarah took lots of photographs of Sam and the team. These two look the same but there are 5 things that are different in picture 2. Can you spot the differences?

ANSWERS: 1. Part of the hose on the roof is missing; 2. The blue light is missing; 3. The dial above Sam's hand is missing; 4. A yellow spot is missing; 5. Elvis's torch is missing.

Can you spot 5 differences in picture 2 of Penny and Venus, the rescue tender?

ANSWERS: 1. The hose is missing; 2. A button is missing; 3. The badge on the door is missing; 4. Part of the front wheel is missing; 5. The tow hook is missing.

Bath-time for Dusty

One day, Station Officer Steele was showing Fireman Sam a painting of a goat.
"That's Idris," Steele told him. "He was the mascot of my old army regiment."

"You know, **we** could do with a station mascot," said Sam.

"Yes," said Steele. "We'll have a mascot that's the pride of Pontypandy, a brave creature, the best beast in Wales! See to it will you, Sam?"

Sarah and James were petting Dusty the dog outside Dilys's shop when she put a notice in the window.

James read it. "Uncle Sam wants a mascot for the Fire Station," he said, looking at Dusty. "And we've got the perfect dog for the job!"

The twins took Dusty to the Fire Station.

"So you reckon Dusty would be the perfect mascot, do you?" said Sam.

"Baaaaa!"

As they were talking, Norman arrived with his pet sheep, Woolly.

"Baaaaa!" said Woolly.

"Norman," warned Sam, "if Station Officer Steele sees that lamb here, he'll ..."

"Make him your mascot!" said Norman, as Woolly jumped out of his arms and raced off.

They found him near the flower boxes at the Fire Station entrance.

"Great fires of London!" said Sam. "He's gobbled up all our geraniums!"

"Great fires of London!"

When Station Officer Steele saw Woolly he said, "Get that sheepskin dustbin away from my station!"

Then he turned to Sam.

"Have you seen Mrs Lasagne's cat, Rosa?" he asked, putting his hand on the flower box. "Bella thinks she would make the perfect mascot."

"Weeeeeooooow!" squealed Rosa, who had been fast asleep in the box.

"Yeeeeeooooow!" cried Steele as she scratched his hand. "That animal is disqualified!"

Sam winked at Sarah and James. "I think Dusty's got a good chance of being the mascot now," he said. "As long as he's cleaned up."

Sarah looked worried. "You mean Dusty needs a ..."

"**BATH?**" said James.

Sam nodded.

When Dusty saw the old tin bath James had filled with water, he whimpered and shook.

"Come on," James told him. "It's only water ..."

ONLY WATER! thought Dusty. What do you mean, **ONLY WATER?**

James held out a dog biscuit to tempt Dusty into the bath but he ran off with it and – **SPLOSH!** – it was James who ended up in the water!

SPLASH! SPLOSH!

Dusty ran away, knocked Norman off his skateboard and rode into the park on it. Then Dusty hit the fountain, soared into the air and landed – **OOF!** – on Trevor, who was taking a nap!

Then he ran off again.

OOF!

The twins chased after Dusty. They thought they'd lost him – when he popped his head out of a dustbin where he had been hiding and ran off again!

"After him!"

Dusty ran to the Mountain Rescue Station, where Mike Flood was repairing a boiler. But his blowtorch started a fire!

When Tom radioed Sam about the fire the alarm bell rang and Sam and Elvis put on their helmets and jumped aboard Jupiter. Her blue light flashed and her siren wailed – **Nee Nah! Nee Nah!** – as they raced to the Mountain Rescue Centre at full speed.

When the fire was out, Steele told the team to damp down the building with their hoses. Just then, Dusty thought it was safe to come out again and got a real soaking.

By the time James and Sarah arrived, water was dripping from his coat.

"Dusty got a bath, after all!" said Sarah.

A few days later, Dusty was dressed in his mascot's outfit. Sarah was trying to take a photograph, but Dusty kept looking away.

"Can someone make him look at the camera?" she asked.

James took a sausage out of his pocket and threw it up into the air. Dusty jumped for it, and when Sarah took the photo, Dusty was too close – and Sam wasn't in the picture at all!

"Oh, Dusty!" said Sam and the others.

"**Woof!**" said Dusty.

"Woof!"

29

Naughty Norman

Dilys Price sells all sorts of things in her shop, from tins of beans to potatoes to mops to ... footballs!

Norman Price would rather play football than help his mum in the shop! Can you help? How many of each thing can you see in the big picture, opposite? Write the numbers in the boxes. Then colour in the big picture.

cans of soup

boxes of eggs

bottles

ANSWERS: 3 cans of soup; 2 boxes of eggs; 3 bottles.

Pizza palaver

One day, Sam and Elvis were on their way back from a rescue when they heard a cry of, "Mamma mia!" It could only be Bella Lasagne!

Sam stopped outside the café where Bella was waving her hands about as Mike Flood tried to push a big object through the door.

"It's-a my-a beautiful new-a pizza oven," Bella told Sam.

"It won't go through the door!" gasped Mike.

"I'll need some rolling pins," Sam told Bella.

Sam laid out the rolling pins, then he and Mike lifted the oven on to them and rolled it into the café!

Bella threw her arms around Sam and gave him a big kiss. **"Grazie! Grazie!"** she said.

Sam smiled as Mike fixed the oven to the chimney. "All part of the service, Bella!" he said.

"Grazie!"

"Grazie!"

Meanwhile, Norman and Mandy were playing football.
"Watch this," said Norman, kicking the ball high into the air.
It hit an old nest that a bird had built on the edge of Bella's chimney ...
and knocked it down inside!

"Oops!" said Norman.
"We'd better tell Bella," said Mandy.
But when Norman saw the new pizza oven, he forgot all about the nest and the chimney. "How about a test pizza, Bella?" he asked.

"OK," said Bella. "But first I-a need-a some-a tomatoes from-a Sam's-a garden."

Norman and Mandy raced for the door. "We'll get them for you!"

When they got back with the tomatoes Bella lit the pizza oven. She didn't know it, but the flames set fire to the bird's nest in the chimney ...

Norman and Mandy made their pizzas. "I'm going to spin my dough," said Norman. But he spun the dough so fast that it flew off his fingers and landed on Trevor Evans' head!

"**Oof!**" said Trevor. "I've never been served that fast before ..."

"Now we-a cook-a the pizzas," said Bella, sliding them into the oven.

After a few minutes, Trevor sniffed and said, "That smells really ..."

"**SMOKY!**" said Norman and Mandy.

"Mamma mia!" said Bella as the café filled with smoke. "Something is-a wrong!"

"Everybody out!" said Trevor. "I'm calling the fire brigade!"

"Everybody out!"

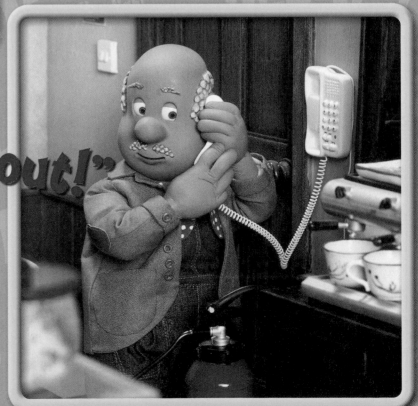

"What a hero!"

Station Officer Steele took the message. "Bella's chimney's on fire. **ACTION STATIONS!**" he said.

The alarm bell rang and Sam and Elvis put on their helmets and jumped aboard Jupiter.

When they got to the café, Bella and the others were watching from outside Dilys's shop. "Mamma mia!" said Bella. "My-a café, she's in-a flames!"

"It's the chimney, Sam," said Trevor.

"We'll have to tackle the fire from above," said Sam calmly as he stood on the platform. "Stabilise Jupiter and extend the Simon snorkel, Elvis!"

The snorkel lifted Sam in place over the chimney. "Water on, Elvis!" Sam called. He pointed the hose down the chimney and the fire was soon out.

"What a hero!" said Dilys.

"Arrrrgh!"

Later on when the café had been cleaned up, Sam showed Bella the old bird's nest. "That was the problem," he told her. "The oven will work fine now."

Sam was right! A little later Bella put four perfect pizzas on the table.

One for Dilys.

One for Sam.

One for Mandy.

One for Norman.

Naughty Norman sprinkled some red-hot chillies on his mum's pizza but Sam saw him and switched the plates when Norman wasn't looking.

When Norman took a **BIG** bite of pizza he chewed, then gasped and pulled a face. "**Arrrrgh!**" he cried. "Now my mouth's on fire!"

Action Stations!

The men and women of the Pontypandy emergency services all know how important it is to work as a team. The vehicles are part of the team, too.

Can you draw lines to match the drivers to their vehicles?

Helen

Venus

Sam

Rescue helicopter

Penny

Jupiter

Tom

Rescue car

38

Now colour in the picture of Tom's Mountain Rescue jeep as neatly as you can. The little picture will help you choose the right colours.

Fun run

One morning, Station Officer Steele was reading his newspaper when Woolly, Norman's pet lamb, chewed a hole straight through it.

"**Baaaaaa!**" said Woolly.

"That walking dustbin's eaten my newspaper!" said Steele.

Norman pushed Woolly away. "I came to ask Sam for an entry form for the fun run," he said. "I'm going to win! First prize is one of Bella's **HUGE** chocolate cakes!"

Later on, Sam and Tom were marking out the fun-run route.

"They start at the station, go out into the country, then home again," said Sam.

"That's it," said Tom as he put up the last of the red paper arrows that would show the runners the way.

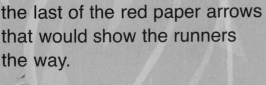

On the day of the race, the runners lined up outside the Fire Station.
"Starting positions, please!" said Sam.
The runners were all getting ready – except Naughty Norman. He ducked down and tied Sarah and James's shoelaces together!
"Remember, follow the red arrows," said Sam. "Ready? On your marks, get set, GO!"

"Hee! Hee!"

Sarah and James took one step, then tripped. "Oh, no!"

Sam untied them and they set off again but Norman and Mandy were a long way ahead. Then Norman raced away from Mandy.

Soon, Norman stopped for a rest. He saw one of the big red arrows and smiled a sneaky smile, as he turned the arrow round! "Hee, hee!" he said. "That will send the others the wrong way!"

He did the same thing with the next arrow.

But when Norman found another arrow it was in Woolly's mouth. "Oh, no!" said Norman. "You've eaten it!" Now **HE** didn't know which way to go!

A little way behind, Sarah, James and Mandy followed the arrows Norman had moved. They climbed over walls and stiles and ran through hedges and muddy puddles.

Back at the station, Sam was getting worried. "Norman, Mandy and the twins are very late. Something's wrong," he told Station Officer Steele.

"We'll send out a search party," said Steele. "**ACTION STATIONS!**"

The alarm bell rang and Sam and Elvis put on their helmets. Then they jumped aboard Jupiter and her blue lights flashed and her siren wailed – **Nee Nah! Nee Nah!** – as they raced off at full speed.

Sam used the radio to call out Tom, and minutes later the rescue helicopter lifted off.

Norman was having a rest in an old shed when Mandy and Sarah arrived, carrying James. "An arrow pointed up a tree so I climbed it," said James. "But I fell."

Norman gulped. "Now who would turn those arrows round?" he asked nervously.

"Who said anything about turning arrows round?" said Mandy. "Norman Price, you're a little cheat!"

"I can explain," said Norman, then he pointed. "Look, it's Tom's helicopter!"

They waved and shouted but Tom didn't see them and flew away.

"He's gone," said James. "Norman, if you hadn't turned the arrows round, we wouldn't be in this mess!"

"**ARROWS!**" said Mandy. "That's it! Right, everyone, collect as many sticks and twigs as you can." She had an idea.

When Tom flew over again he spoke to Sam on the radio. "I've just spotted a giant arrow made of sticks near the old shed!"

"We'll meet you there," said Sam.

"Look, it's Tom's helicopter!"

"Sam!"

Mandy was **VERY** pleased to see them!
So was Sarah.
So was James.
So was Norman.
So was Woolly.

Sam sat James on his knee. "We'd better get back and let Nurse Flood take a look at your ankle," he told him.

Soon, he and the others – even Woolly! – were speeding back to Pontypandy aboard Jupiter.

Later, in Bella's café, Station Officer Steele gave out the the fun-run prizes.

"There are three winners," he said. "Mandy, Sarah and James get Bella's chocolate cake."

"And there's one of my home-made cup cakes for Norman, the runner-up," said Elvis Cridlington, proudly.

Elvis's cakes looked more like rocks, so Norman gave his to Woolly.

Usually Woolly eats **ANYTHING** – but not this time! He spat out the cake and stuck out his tongue: **"Baaaaaa! Urgh!"**

The hero next door

Draw over the lines to copy the picture of Sam and Jupiter. It's easy if you do it square by square. You could colour in the picture, then write your name on the line.

These are the colours you need:

 Sam and Jupiter by _____

47

Joker Soaker

You can help read this story about Naughty Norman. Listen to the words and when you see a picture, say the name.

One hot, dry day a parcel arrives

for . Inside is a giant Joker

Soaker water pistol.  fills it

with water and fires it at .

"Don't waste water in this dry

weather!" says .

Next,  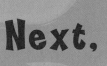 throws a coin at 's

feet. He bends down to pick it up and

 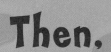 fires water at his bottom!

Then,  fires his water pistol at

 and . When  goes

to the Fire Station to fill it up again,

 is waiting for him!

"Don't waste water, !" says

. But  just laughs and runs

off. In the park,  is going to

soak  when he stops.

's head is stuck in the railings!

Poor  is hot and thirsty, so

fires water into his mouth instead.

When  and  see

they call , who soon cuts

 free.  asks if he can look

at the Joker Soaker and  hands

it to him.  fires the Joker Soaker

at . "Ugh!" says . "Now

I'M soaked!"

Sam to the rescue!

Sam is always the first on the scene in an emergency!
Which pieces are missing from the jigsaw pictures of Sam?
Draw in the missing pieces, then colour them in.

52

2

a

b

c

d

e

f

53

It was the morning of Fireman Sam's birthday, but when the post arrived there were no cards for him, not even one from Sarah and James. Sam felt a bit sad.

Sam's friends hadn't really forgotten his birthday. They had cards and presents for him and were planning a secret **surprise party** that afternoon in the Fire Station gym!

Norman's job was to keep Sam away from the Fire Station until one o'clock.

Bella was decorating Sam's birthday cake when Norman arrived with some candles. "Take extra care with them because Mam says ..." he said.

"Mamma mia!" said Bella. "Shh! Sam is-a coming!"

Bella hid the cake and Norman said, "Er, where are you going, Sam?"

"I'm off to the Fire Station," said Sam.

"Oh, no, you're not!" thought Norman and he ran to the park. He threw some dog chews for Dusty into the fountain just as Sam walked by.

"Dusty's in the fountain and he can't swim!" cried Norman.

But Dusty jumped out and knocked Norman into the water!

"I thought Dusty was in the fountain," said Sam.

"He was," said Norman. "But I ... er ... rescued him!"

Sam helped Norman out of the fountain and they walked to the Fire Station together.

But when they got there, Elvis said they couldn't come in!

"Why not?" asked Sam.

"Because you've got to ... say the password!" said Norman.

"Er, that's right," said Elvis. "Special security, see."

"But I don't know the password," said Sam.

"You could guess," suggested Norman.

Sam sighed. "Oh, all right. 'Fountain'?"

"No."

"'Cappuccino'?"

"No," said Elvis, shaking his head.

While Sam carried on guessing Norman slipped inside. "Sam's coming!" he cried.

"Put everything in the gym!" said Sarah.

Norman went back outside.

"'Dusty'?" said Sam.

"Correct!" said Elvis. "Come in, Sam."

"Oh, no!" thought Norman. It was still too soon for Sam to go into the gym. Norman had to do something – quickly!

"Cappuccino?"

"Oo-er ..." he said, going all wobbly. "I feel funny!"

Sam took Norman home, but as soon as Sam had gone Norman made a very quick recovery.

"Party time!" he said.

In the café Bella and Mandy were testing the candles.
They lit them then blew them out. But these were no
ordinary candles – when Bella and Mandy went into the
kitchen, the flames lit up again!

When Norman and Dusty arrived, Dusty tried to lick Sam's cake. It slid off the table, but not before the candles had set the curtains on fire!

"Help!" cried Norman.

"Mamma mia!" said Bella. "Everybody out!"

"SURPRISE!"

"Happy birthday, Sam!"

"**ACTION STATIONS!**" said Station Officer Steele when he heard about the fire.

The alarm bell rang and Sam and Elvis jumped aboard Jupiter with her blue lights flashing and her siren wailing – **Nee Nah! Nee Nah!** – and they raced off at full speed.

They soon put out the fire.

Bella made a new cake for Sam and later, at the Fire Station, the party was ready. Norman called Sam into the gym.

"**SURPRISE!**" cried everyone. "Happy birthday, Sam!"

"I thought you'd forgotten," said Sam.

"Course not," said Sarah. "We had to get everything ready in secret."

"And it was my job to keep you out of here," said Norman.

"Blow out the candles on your cake, Sam," said Elvis.

Sam did just that – but the candles lit up again!

"Crikey, Sam," said Norman. "You must be getting old. You haven't got enough puff to blow out your candles!"

Nee Nah! Nee Nah!

Fireman Sam has been called out to another emergency.
He has to make sure that he takes all sorts of equipment with him,
he never knows what he might need.
Which of the things on these pages should Sam take with him?
Write a ✓ or a ✗ in each box.

ANSWERS: Sam should take the fire extinguisher, the torch, the bucket, the walkie-talkies and the metal cutters.

Let it snow

It was nearly Christmas and Pontypandy lay under a soft white snowy blanket.

When Mandy and Norman went to decorate the Christmas tree, Sam had some bad news. "Sorry," he said. "There are no trees left at the garden centre."

"But Christmas isn't Christmas without a tree!" said Norman.

The weather got worse and worse. Trevor set off to Newtown to try to collect things for the villagers – including a Christmas tree. But he couldn't get through: the road was blocked!

That afternoon, Mandy and Norman set off with a sledge.

"We'll get a tree from Pontypandy Mountain," said Norman. "But we need a husky to pull us there. I know – Dusty!"

Soon he was tied to the sledge, but poor Dusty couldn't pull them both.

"You go without me," said Mandy.

"Right," said Norman. "See you back at the Fire Station. Come on, Dusty, MUSH!"

Dilys told Fireman Sam about the road. "We're cut off!" she said. "I haven't got any food left in my shop for customers."

"Don't worry," said Sam, taking out his mobile. "Tom will help."

Up on Pontypandy Mountain, Norman was singing "Oh what fun it is to ride on a one-dog open sleigh", when Dusty ran under some low branches and Norman ended up with a long snowy beard, just like Santa!

"Ho, ho!" laughed Norman.

He tried to pull up a little fir tree but the ground was frozen and it wouldn't budge. "STUPID THING!" said Norman loudly.

Suddenly, snow started to slip down the mountain. Norman was pushed into a cave and the entrance was blocked!

"HELP!" cried Naughty Norman.

"Ho, ho!"

"HELP!"

63

Dusty escaped and pulled home the empty sledge. When Mandy saw him, she told Dilys that Norman had gone up the mountain.

"He'll freeze without a vest!" said Dilys. "I'll phone the Station."

"**ACTION STATIONS!**" said Station Officer Steele when he took the message. "Norman Price is missing on Pontypandy Mountain!"

The alarm bell rang and Sam and Elvis jumped aboard Jupiter, with her blue lights flashing and her siren wailing – **Nee Nah! Nee Nah!** – as they raced off at full speed.

Sam stopped at Dilys's shop. "We need someone with a good nose to find Norman," he said. "We need Dusty and we need him now!"

Up on the mountain Sam said, "Right, Dusty. Show us where Norman is."

Dusty set off, nose to the ground. He stopped outside the cave. "**Woof! Woof!**" said Dusty.

"Start digging!" said Sam.

"Brrrr!"

Inside the cave, Norman was very cold. He was walking up and down, trying to keep warm, when a shovel cut through the wall of snow.

"Sam, is that you?" Norman shouted. "Hurry up, my bum's gone numb!"

Sam soon got Norman out of the cave. He was **VERY** pleased to see Sam – and Dusty.

Back home, Sam warned Norman not to go off on his own again.

"But I had to get a Christmas tree for the village," said Norman.

"Three cheers for Dusty!"

"Hip, hip, hurray!"

Just then, Tom's helicopter hovered above them. He had brought food for the villagers and a long string of fairy lights, which he dropped on to a tall tree.

"Look, Mam!" said Norman. "We've got a Christmas tree, after all!"

That night, everyone went to look at the Christmas tree.

"Here, Dusty," said Norman, giving him a big bone. "This is for rescuing me. Three cheers for Dusty! **Hip, hip, hurray!**"

Testing, testing!

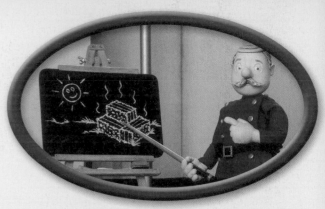

"**TESTING STATIONS!** Try my quiz to see how much you know about Fireman Sam and the Pontypandy Fire Service. You can check your answers at the bottom of the page."

1 What are the names of Sam's niece and nephew?

2 Who does Rosa the cat belong to?

3 In the story "Let it snow" who led Sam to the cave where Norman was stuck?

4 Who is this making a fuss of Norman?

5 Sam is the cook at Pontypandy fire station. True or false?

6 Who drives the Pontypandy bus?

7 Who pretended to be an alien from Venus?

8 Who drives Venus the rescue tender?

9 This is the Pontypandy odd-job man. What is his name?

10 Who is the pilot of the Mountain Rescue Service helicopter? Is it:

a Tom Thomas
b Trevor Evans
c Penny Morris?

68

ANSWERS: 1. James and Sarah; 2. Bella Lasagne; 3. Dusty; 4. His mum, Dilys Price; 5. False – it's Elvis Cridlington; 6. Trevor Evans; 7. Naughty Norman Price; 8. Penny Morris; 9. Mike Flood; 10. a, Tom Thomas.

Nee Nah! Nee Nah! Nee Nah!

Use your best crayons to colour me in!

Action Stations!

For more colouring fun, look out for Fireman Sam in his own magazine ...

FREE Binoculars

Fireman Sam NEW

Issue 1

Puzzles • Posters • Activities

Free gift with every issue!

Coming soon to all good newsagents and supermarkets

Don't miss it!